SPOOKY SMACKDOWN

BY KNIFE & PACKER

Kane Miller
A DIVISION OF EDC PUBLISHING

First American Edition 2015
Kane Miller, A Division of EDC Publishing

Text and illustrations copyright © Knife and Packer 2014
First published by Scholastic Australia, a division of Scholastic Australia Pty Limited in 2014
This edition published under license from Scholastic Australia Pty Limited.

For information contact:
Kane Miller, A Division of EDC Publishing
P.O. Box 470663
Tulsa, OK 74147-0663
www.kanemiller.com
www.edcpub.com
www.usbornebooksandmore.com

Library of Congress Control Number: 2014950515

Manufactured by Regent Publishing Services, Hong Kong
Printed March 2015 in ShenZhen, Guangdong, China

Paperback ISBN: 978-1-61067-396-9
Hardcover ISBN: 978-1-61067-432-4

MEET THE WHEELNUTS!

Rust Bucket 3000

UPGRADE!
11
giant chopping tool

The Rust Bucket 3000 is the most high-tech robot car in the universe. Driven by super-sophisticated robots Nutz and Boltz, this team is always happy to use robo-gadgets to get ahead of the opposition.

The Wheel Deal

Dustin Grinner and Myley Twinkles aren't just car drivers, they are actually super-cheesy pop singers and stars of daytime TV. The Wheel Deal, their super-souped-up stretch limo, is showbiz on wheels!

UPGRADE!
8
fireworks display

Dino-Wagon

This prehistoric car is driven by the Dino-Crew—Turbo Rex and Flappy, a pterodactyl and all-around nervous passenger. Powered by an active volcano, this vehicle has a turbo boost unlike anything seen on Earth!

UPGRADE!
10
ice cream freezer

The Flying Diaper

Babies are great, but they are also gross, and nothing could be more gross than this pair. Gurgle and Burp are a duo of high-speed babies whose gas-powered Flying Diaper can go from zero to gross out in seconds!

UPGRADE! 5 baby food

The Supersonic Sparkler

Petrolnella and Dieselina (known as Nelly and Dee-Dee) are fairies with attitude, and with a sprinkling of fairy dust, the Supersonic Sparkler has a surprising turn of speed.

UPGRADE! 6 super-drying magic powder

The Jumping Jalopy

This grandfather and grandson team drive a not-always-reliable 1930s Bugazzi. Although determined to win on skill alone, they are not above some "old-school cunning" to keep in the race.

UPGRADE! 7 woolly undies

3

CHAPTER 1

High in the mountains, in a town square surrounded by spooky buildings, haunted castles and ghoulish roads, multibillionaire Warren "Wheelie" Wheelnut had gathered the most amazing collection of cars ever. Welcome to **Spookytania**, home of the scariest racetrack on Earth!

As with the start of all Wheelnut races, a large crowd was there to cheer—but if you looked closely you could see this was no ordinary crowd.

"Howdy, ladies and gentlemen, boys and girls—or should I say ghouls and ghosts, phantoms and spirits?" said Wheelie. "Welcome to the second 'Wheelnuts! Craziest Race on Earth!'" The whole spooky crowd went wild. "The rules are simple—there *are no* rules!" he continued. "Now let me introduce you to the Wheelnuts themselves!"

As the cars revved up their engines, Wheelie introduced each team and asked them what they thought of the haunted course.

"First up we have the Dino-Wagon!"

Any ghost in *our* way will find this team has got teeth!

And wings!

"Next, the Wheel Deal!"

We would actually *love* to get some ghosts into our next dance routine ...

"Over here we have the Flying Diaper!"

We buoooooooooooorp in the face of fear!

"Next up, the Supersonic Sparkler!"

Any ghosts want to get lively? We've got the fairy dust to make it a bust!

"Say hello to the Rust Bucket 3000!"

We've driven the haunted galaxy of Spookulon 7!

Our sensors do not detect fear!

Fear? We eat fear for breakfast!

With terror for lunch!

"And last, but by no means least, we have the Jumping Jalopy!"

So there we have it folks, please give a *Wheelie* big round of applause for the Wheelnuts!

"Racing is all about winning and we have big shiny trophies for the top three drivers," said Wheelie. "Plus there are Wheelnut Gold Stars to be won at checkpoints and in the world-famous Wheelnut Challenge. You can use these stars at the Wheelnut Garage to buy gadgets, cheats or car upgrades! So there's no excuse to go gently on this ghostly track!"

DONG!

DONG!

It was time for the race to start. Wheelie climbed to the top of the tallest, scariest bell tower. The cars growled and roared as they got ready to go.

Wheelie poked his head out from the top of the bell tower.

"I'm so excited I think even my moustache may be haunted! Now let's get out there and get driving!!!" he bellowed, before he rang the church bell.

The Wheelnuts shuddered to the tips of their exhaust pipes as the bell's peal boomed across town … and the contestants were off!

The ghostly crowd went crazy as the cars screeched out of the town center and through the narrow cobbled streets. The Flying Diaper locked wheels with the Dino-Wagon, the Supersonic Sparkler almost upended the Rust Bucket 3000 and, taking an early lead, was the Jumping Jalopy.

VA-ROOM!

But before they even hit the first turn disaster struck! .

One problem with having a ghostly crowd was that they could simply walk *through* the metal barriers lining the route. As if that wasn't bad enough, one of the ghosts had dropped something very important onto the track—his head! As it bounced along the road the Jumping Jalopy was the first to spot it …

"A head!" shouted James.

"I'm trying to get ahead!" exclaimed Campbell.

"No, Grandad, a *real* head! We've got to get it off the track before it causes a pileup," said James. "I've got an idea—drive as close to it as you can, then hold on to my feet!"

"Galloping gear sticks!" said Campbell as he tried to slow down.

Using all his racing driver skills, Campbell managed to pull the Jumping Jalopy in line with the head.

As the head took a big bounce James reached up, grabbed it and in one slick move took aim and shot it through the air—straight back onto the owner's neck!

"Great basketball skills!" shouted Campbell just as the Rust Bucket 3000, the Dino-Wagon and the Wheel Deal all screeched up behind them. "That was close—now let's get out of town and race!"

CHAPTER 2

Having narrowly avoided a ghost's head the Wheelnuts could concentrate on what they did best—racing! In seconds they were out of the town and powering downhill—fast!

The town was built on the top of an incredibly steep mountain. The road down was very narrow with a sheer drop to one side—and no roadside barriers. Some of the Wheelnuts were loving it!

The Jumping Jalopy was still in the lead.

"Don't you just LOVE the fresh mountain air! And the views—I could stare at them all day!" Campbell said, taking his eyes off the road and looking out over the mountaintops.

"Please don't do that!" exclaimed James as the Bugazzi swerved dangerously close to the edge!

SCREECH!

Campbell had to concentrate on the road because the other cars were closing in fast. In fact, the Wheel Deal was right behind them and cheesy pop stars Dustin Grinner and Myley Twinkles seemed to be in their element.

"When you have performed in front of as many people as we have, you just don't get nervous!" said Dustin. But then Myley swung the car around a particularly tight corner and Dustin's fur hat came flying off and tumbled down the mountainside.

BOINK!

"Wardrobe malfunction!" wailed the pop wannabe. "Abandon race!"

As the Wheel Deal pulled over the other cars screeched past. The Rust Bucket 3000, which had moved into second place, seemed to be missing its codriver.

"What are you doing, Boltz?!" said Nutz. "I need some help here!"

"By my calculations any fall from this height would result in severe robot structure failure," wailed Boltz, cowering in a corner and covering his eyes.

Just then the Dino-Wagon burst into view.

"There is only one way to handle these steep parts," said Turbo Rex. "Close your eyes, hold tight and splatter the competition with ice cream!" (The Dino-Wagon had used their Gold Stars from the first race to buy an onboard ice cream freezer.)

"That's easy for you to say!" wailed a terrified Flappy as they lurched towards the Supersonic Sparkler. "Take that!"

"Ha-ha, you can't beat us!" cackled Turbo Rex as the Sparkler's windshield was covered by chocolate ice cream. "Your turn, throw your nastiest fairy dust at us!"

But for once the Supersonic Sparkler didn't have any suitable magic dust to respond with.

The Wheelnuts finally reached the valley at the foot of the mountain.

"Phew," said Gurgle. "A flat part—I thought my diaper was going to explode!"

Soon they entered a small forest.

"What on earth could happen in a forest?" chortled Burp. But there was a rustle in the undergrowth, a growl in the bushes and the blinking of eyes in the treetops …

CHAPTER 3

The Wheelnuts had just entered **Spookytania's Haunted Forest!** Even the trees were haunted—their branches had completely blocked the path.

But one car wasn't bothered by how creepy the place was—the Rust Bucket 3000.

"This place reminds me of Balbulian Forests in the Narkattack Nebula," said Nutz. "Time to use a robo-gadget!"

Boltz pressed a button on the control panel and a large robotic arm appeared.

It was a giant robotic chopping tool and it was soon hacking a path through the **Haunted Forest.**

"Hold tight!" cried Nutz as they built up speed. "See you later, losers!"

As the Rust Bucket 3000 sped through the forest the other Wheelnuts did their best to keep up. But one vehicle had dropped quite a long way behind. The Supersonic Sparkler duo seemed to have their minds on matters other than leading the race.

Unlike the other racers who couldn't wait to get out of the creepy forest, Dee-Dee and Nelly needed to get deeper into it!

"The path has got to be along here somewhere," said Dee-Dee as the car's antennae tried to pick up the right direction.

"That's the trouble with haunted woods, the trees keep walking all over the place," said Nelly.

They were about to give up when Dee-Dee noticed a small wooden sign, pointing to an even narrower, scarier-looking path!

"This must be it," said Nelly as the car did its best to navigate the narrow lane. And finally, there before them was the place they were looking for.

"The Wood Goblin Fairy Supply Store!" said Dee-Dee as they hopped out of the car. "Time to top up all our magic fairy dusts!"

While Nelly and Dee-Dee choose their magic fairy dusts let's take a closer look at their car as we put the Supersonic Sparkler UNDER THE SPOTLIGHT!

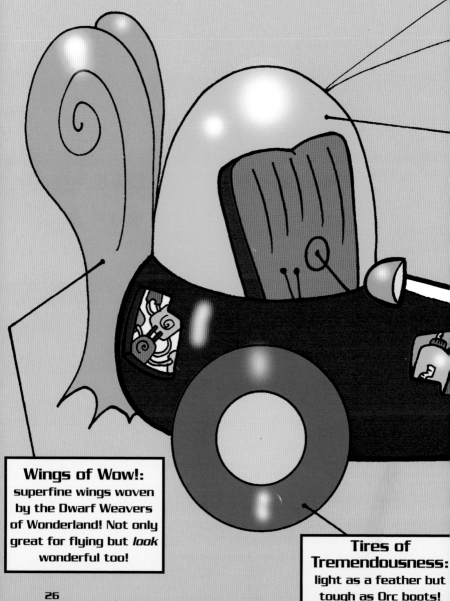

Wings of Wow!: superfine wings woven by the Dwarf Weavers of Wonderland! Not only great for flying but *look* wonderful too!

Tires of Tremendousness: light as a feather but tough as Orc boots!

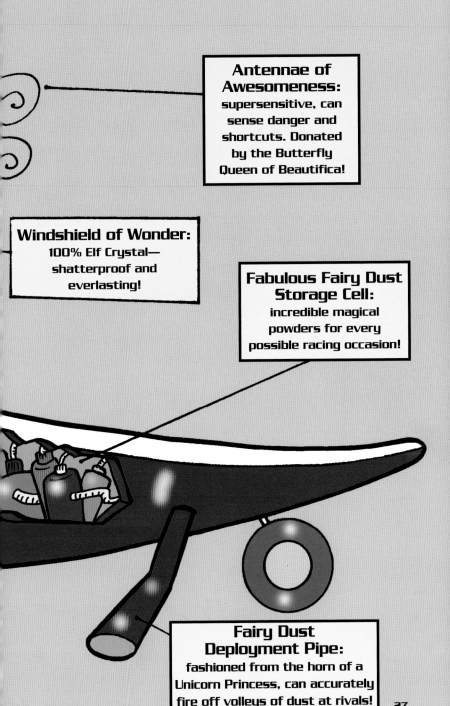

Antennae of Awesomeness: supersensitive, can sense danger and shortcuts. Donated by the Butterfly Queen of Beautifica!

Windshield of Wonder: 100% Elf Crystal—shatterproof and everlasting!

Fabulous Fairy Dust Storage Cell: incredible magical powders for every possible racing occasion!

Fairy Dust Deployment Pipe: fashioned from the horn of a Unicorn Princess, can accurately fire off volleys of dust at rivals!

But the storekeeper had bad news:

"I'm afraid we're completely out of tickling dust, sneezing dust, tire-melt dust and we've not had any engine-malfunction dust in weeks."

"How can we cheat, er, I mean compete in the race without magic fairy dust?" wailed Dee-Dee.

"You have no idea how sneaky those other drivers can be," said Nelly.

"I'll get them to you as soon as I can," said the goblin.

CHAPTER 4

Back on the track the Supersonic Sparkler had some ground to make up. Fortunately its fairy wings meant that the car could fly for short bursts.

"Time to flap!" said Dee-Dee, pressing the Turbo Flap button.

"And ... flap!" said Nelly as the car took off. Tall branches reached out and tried to grab them.

The Sparkler was starting to lose altitude as they finally caught up with the rest of the racers. The road started to clear—with small shrubs rather than trees trying to grab at the racers. The race was back on!

Up ahead, right next to the track, were a pair of huge toadstools, one tall and gangly, the other short and squat. Both had arms and they were speaking to each other.

On closer inspection it was clear these were people in toadstool disguises! Warren Wheelnut's evil twin brother, Waylon "Wipeout" Wheelnut, and his sidekick, Dipstick, who were watching and plotting.

"I can hear them coming," said Wipeout. "So they can cope with haunted trees, can they? Well will they be able to cope with what *I've* got ready for them?"

Unlike his twin brother, Wipeout was not a popular, successful billionaire. Which was why his main mission in life was to wreck his brother's race!

"Everything is in place, Mr. Wipeout, sir!" chuckled Dipstick. "The dragon will be in position any minute—and what a beast it is!"

"Perfect—a dragon! Now that's what I call scary," said Wipeout.

Just then the race leaders appeared …

The Rust Bucket 3000 was still in first place, but only just. Right behind them was the Flying Diaper and in third was the Supersonic Sparkler, which had recovered well from its stop for fairy dust.

"Look at these four-wheeled fools!" said Wipeout as the first three cars sped past. "They don't even know we're here!"

"They have no idea what's in store for them!" cackled Dipstick.

The next group of cars sped past—the Wheel Deal, the Dino-Wagon and the Jumping Jalopy.

But as Wipeout and Dipstick were getting ready to leave they heard an engine—one of the cars was reversing back down the road towards them! The Dino-Wagon was making an unscheduled pit stop.

"I know the race is important," said Turbo Rex, "but there are some delicacies you can't turn your snout up at."

Wipeout and Dipstick had no idea what the dinosaur drivers were after until it was too late …

"I've not seen such a delicious-looking snack in about 30,000 years," said Flappy.

"And I am rav-en-ous!" said Turbo Rex.

The villains had to use all their powers of concentration not to scream as Turbo Rex and Flappy took great bites from their toadstool legs.

"This is disgusting!" said Turbo Rex, spitting out the chunk of fake toadstool.

"It tastes really plastic-y," said Flappy. "No more snacking in these woods—let's get back on track!"

As the Dino-Wagon zoomed back into the race, Wipeout and Dipstick hobbled away to get the next part of their evil plan underway.

CHAPTER 5

With the **Haunted Forest** behind them, the Wheelnuts found themselves driving along a straight road that went through a large flat plain. In the distance they could see a gateway that led to a bridge—the first checkpoint! At first the scenery looked like any countryside, but in **Spookytania** nothing is quite as it seems: the farms were creepy, the animals were ghostly and even the crops seemed sinister.

The drivers were getting used to this kind of thing though, and with no trees and plants to get in their way they could finally get down to some real racing!

The first to make a move was the Jumping Jalopy …

"Ah, the open road! Nothing to get in our way except the occasional spooky animal. Time to hit the front!" said Campbell as he drove straight through a startled-looking herd of ghost cows. "Now!"

James used all his strength to crank the Bugazzi's ancient gear stick into top gear. With a final big effort the car lurched and they shot into the lead.

"Yi-haaa!" chortled Campbell as a flock of zombie chickens scattered.

The cars behind them were soon doing their best to catch up … the Dino-Wagon was hitting top speed and the Rust Bucket 3000 was jostling the Wheel Deal. But one of the cars was now plotting something spectacular … the Flying Diaper.

"We are in last place—perfect," said Gurgle. "Time for something HUGE!"

"You don't mean …" gulped Burp.

"You'd better believe it," said Gurgle. "Spoon in position and—aim …"

Now, as we mentioned before, in the Craziest Race on Earth there are no rules, and what was about to happen is not something we will make excuses for. So if you're easily offended, look away now—because on the next page is a "SUPER-SICK MEGA-NAUGHTY CHEAT."

SUPER-SICK MEGA-NAUGHTY CHEAT!

The terrible twosome pressed a button and a large plastic spoon unleashed THE BABY FOOD TYPHOON—a torrent of gross-out baby food! All the other cars were now stuck in horrible, sticky, smelly, baby food!

KER-SPLAT!

"Oh this is just too un-fluffy!" wailed Dee-Dee in the Supersonic Sparkler.

"This is worse than being slimed on a game show!" warbled Myley in the Wheel Deal.

The Flying Diaper giggled all the way past the stricken Wheelnuts.

"Checkpoint here we come!" laughed Burp.

As the cheating babies sped up the road the rest of the drivers had to figure out how to get out of the sticky food—and fast!

First out was the Supersonic Sparkler.

The Wheel Deal tried to shake off the baby food by turning the sound system up to max, but that didn't work and they had to get out and push.

James and Campbell were having to do the same with the Jumping Jalopy.

The Dino-Wagon was using a pair of pterodactyls to try to get it up and out.

But the Rust Bucket 3000 was in big trouble. If there's one thing robots can't take it's rust ...

CHAPTER 6

The Flying Diaper crossed the bridge in first place, the Supersonic Sparkler crossed next and then the other cars all sped across. On the other side of the bridge was a HUGE castle—and not the friendly-looking sort!

The Wheelnuts were at the first race checkpoint.

"Howdy, drivers—some of you look like you just saw a ghost!" greeted Wheelie. "Congratulations on some mighty fine driving … and cheatin'! Let's take a look at who won how many stars!"

The stars: 6 stars for first place, 5 stars for second place, 4 stars for third place, 3 stars for fourth place, 2 stars for fifth place and 1 star for sixth place.

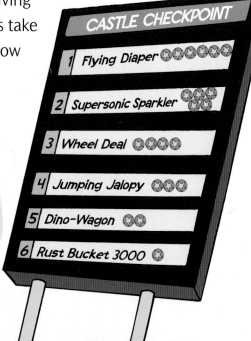

CASTLE CHECKPOINT

1 Flying Diaper ⭐⭐⭐⭐⭐⭐

2 Supersonic Sparkler ⭐⭐⭐⭐⭐

3 Wheel Deal ⭐⭐⭐⭐

4 Jumping Jalopy ⭐⭐⭐

5 Dino-Wagon ⭐⭐

6 Rust Bucket 3000 ⭐

The drivers knew what was coming next—the "Wheelnut Challenge."

"Now you have already seen quite a few ghosts on this race …" said Wheelie as he led the drivers to a huge, heavy wooden door.

"Yeah—and you call *them* scary!" scoffed Gurgle.

"Well, behind this door each team has a ghost specifically designed to be scary to them," said Wheelie.

"This challenge is called the Room of Super-Mega-Help-I-Want-My-Mommy Terror," Wheelie continued.

This got the drivers' attention—it sounded quite a bit scarier than ghost cows and zombie chickens.

"This challenge is all about who can last longest," said Wheelie. "When you've had enough just shout, 'I'm a Wheelnut, get me out of here!'"

GULP!

The huge door creaked open and one by one the drivers nervously stepped through, into the Room of Super-Mega-Help-I-Want-My-Mommy Terror. They were in a large empty room—it wasn't dark and it wasn't scary—yet.

"There's nothing in here!" said Boltz.

"Let's just kick back and relax," said Flappy.

Then James noticed something in the far end of the room—there were six dusty old bottles, each labeled with a different team name.

"These are addressed to us," said James. "Time to meet our ghosts!"

The contestants opened their bottles and what came out was even scarier than they feared!

James and Campbell were faced with a huge human figure—but this was no ordinary figure—it was actually a school principal—a ghost school principal!

The Dino-Wagon team were faced with the *smallest* ghost they had ever seen.

The Supersonic Sparkler crew was being chased
by a fluff-eating hobgoblin.

The Robots had a rust demon haunting them.

The only drivers still in the Room of Super-Mega-Help-I-Want-My-Mommy Terror were the Flying Diaper and the Wheel Deal. Unlike the others, they seemed to enjoy having their own ghosts!

The Terrible Two were being haunted by a giant, angry mommy!

And the Wheel Deal were faced with a showbiz-hating, CD-, DVD- and MP3-eating ghoul!

It was a case of who was going to crack first. Unfortunately, the ghost mommy was about to scare the life out of Gurgle and Burp …

That's it! Bath time!

Bath? Never! I'm a Wheelnut, get me out of here!

The last team standing was the Wheel Deal—they just love an audience, even a haunted audience that hates all music!

OK, Mr. Ghoul—you don't like music? We'll try some pop poetry on you …

And if that doesn't work we have a three-hour modern dance routine we just know you're going to love …

I'm a ghoul, get me out of here!

The challenge was over and the drivers reassembled by their cars. After all the scariness of the Room of Super-Mega-Help-I-Want-My-Mommy Terror everyone was relieved to be back in the spooky castle!

"Congratulations to the Wheel Deal—they have been given 5 bonus Gold Stars for winning the Challenge."

CHAPTER 7

With the Wheelnut Challenge behind them, it was time to start racing again. But as always, Warren Wheelnut had a surprise for the drivers.

"The next stage of the race is an *indoor* stage!" said the eccentric billionaire. "You'll notice that everything in this castle looks a bit big. That's because it's a **giant's** castle! Good luck!"

The drivers were taking on the strangest part of the race yet.

At first the Wheelnuts were all neck and neck as they went through a series of rooms.

"So far, so clear of ghosts," said Nelly.

"So far," said Dee-Dee, who had noticed what lay ahead. A long sweeping staircase, lined with suits of armor. Suits of armor that looked decidedly haunted.

"This is going to test the Bugazzi's suspension," said Campbell as they looked up at the stairs. "Hold tight!"

The haunted suits of armor started disrupting the race—swishing swords tried to swipe at the cars as they sped past. One team hated this ...

"Not the hair!" wailed Myley. "I have my own stylist!"

"Do you have any idea how much this suit cost!" complained Dustin.

SWOOSH!

SWIPE!

While others seemed to be enjoying it ...

"Hey, they're trying to high-five us! Cool!" gurgled Burp.

But the team least able to cope was the Dino-Wagon, who were in last place—it seemed the volcano had acquired some passengers.

"Help!" squealed Flappy. "There's half an army in here!"

"Time for some dino-power!" said Turbo Rex as she set the volcano to "HOT." There was some loud squealing before half a dozen big, hot-and-bothered ghost knights came jumping out.

At the top of the stairs the cars had to drive through a vast bathroom full of toxic fumes. Plus there was something in there—something alive!

"Hey, get your foot off the brake!" yelled Nelly, noticing that they were now almost stationary.

"My foot's not on the brake," said Dee-Dee.

It was only when they looked in the wing mirror that they realized a large tentacle was holding on to them. A tentacle that was coming out of the toilet!

"OK, this is a problem," said Nelly. "We're being pulled back towards the toilet … do something!"

"Like what?" screeched Dee-Dee, who was just as horrified by what was happening.

Fortunately at that moment the Jumping Jalopy appeared. With the path out of the bathroom blocked, urgent action was needed.

"Right, I've never had to tackle a toilet ghost before," said Campbell. "We need to be cunning, we need to think this through from every angle."

"Or we could just flush," said James, who had bravely hopped out. He dodged the tentacles until there was a loud gurgling noise and the squid was gone.

"Thanks, James," said Dee-Dee, and the race was back on. Up more stairs, along galleries until the exit came into view …

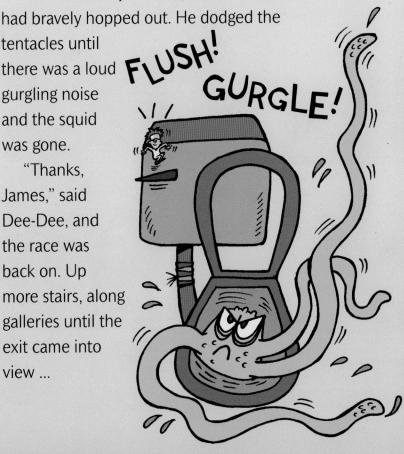

FLUSH! GURGLE!

CHAPTER 8

But outside the castle something even more sinister was happening. Wipeout and Dipstick were high on a mountaintop, waiting.

"They should be out of that silly castle any moment now, Mr. Wipeout, sir," said Dipstick.

"Well if they think *that* place is spooky," chuckled Wipeout, "wait until they get a load of what *we've* got in store for them!"

"The beast is in position and ready to be brought into action!" said Dipstick. Hidden in a cave behind them, something was alive. Something huge!

"My pretty is ready to do what she does best!" cackled Wipeout. "Is it just me or is there a chill in the air?"

"Oh it's getting colder all right," said Dipstick. "It's getting *much* colder!"

CHAPTER 9

The Wheelnuts all burst out through the castle gates, relieved to be back on the open road.

"I think that's the worst behind us," said Campbell as they screeched around the first turn of the track.

"Don't say that, Grandpa!" said James. Campbell had this terrible habit of saying everything was great—just as things got really awful!

And sure enough, something awful was starting to happen …

The sky had gone a strange and sinister color.
"Hey, who turned out the lights?" said Gurgle.
"It's not our bedtime is it?" wailed Burp. "But I
am starting to feel sleepy!"

The sky was getting darker and darker, in fact it
had gotten so dark that the cars all had to pull over—
the race had stopped! As the drivers scratched their
heads and looked up at the sky, one of the teams was
simply NOT going to put up with it …

Myley Twinkles and Dustin Grinner were standing on the roof of the Wheel Deal. "No one turns the lights out on us!" said Myley, the cheesiest superstar ever to race a car.

"*These* stars are going to keep on shining brightly!" added Dustin, equal cheesiest superstar.

"Cover your eyes and expect to be dazzled!" said Myley as she switched on the huge spotlight they kept stored in the trunk of their car.

The drivers winced as the bright light shone in their eyes. But it was their ears that were about to take a pounding …

"Guys—have we got a treat for you!" said Dustin, placing a portable webcam in position.

"Yes—seeing as there is a break in racing we thought we would use the opportunity to record our latest music video!" said Myley. "And broadcast it live on our webcam … Lights, camera—action!"

This was *much* more frightening than anything the course had thrown up so far, and the drivers winced and hid behind their hands.

But just as Dustin and Myley were about to sing the chorus for the sixth time, something flapped down from the sky. Even the Wheel Deal crew had to stop singing as the giant creature flew straight towards the cars.

"The Supersonic Sparkler?" said a pink unicorn.

"Over here! You must be our delivery unicorn!" said Nelly. "And you've got all our powders! Thank you!"

The unicorn placed a huge box of powders on the ground, but as it left it gave a stark warning …

With the unicorn gone, Dee-Dee was able to use some Superbright Twinkly Magic Powder to light up the road and once again the race was underway, even though they were going slowly.

But the dark clouds above now delivered what they had been threatening to—snow, and not just a flake or two but a full-blown blizzard!"

CHAPTER 10

Now, for some racers this was the first time they had ever seen snow. In fact even those racers who had seen snow before had never seen this much snow, and no one was coping very well …

The Dino-Wagon dinosaurs were being pulled by a baby woolly mammoth.

Nutz and Boltz were discovering they had not been built for cold. Nutz had turned the onboard heaters to maximum to try and melt the snow.

The Supersonic Sparkler tried to fly through the snow, but the wings couldn't cope with the cold.

James and Campbell scrambled to shut the roof of their ancient sports car, but it had more holes than Swiss cheese ...

Meanwhile, on board the Flying Diaper, the babies couldn't budge and their usual ever-reliable drool was worse than useless.

Finally, on the Wheel Deal, Dustin and Myley had not only given up on driving, but any hope of keeping warm in the onboard hot tub was dashed.

The race had once again ground to a halt—they simply couldn't get through the snow. But it soon became clear that the snow was not coming from an ordinary snow cloud.

"What is that shape up on the hill?" asked James.

"I don't know, but it looks suspicious even for this place," said Flappy. "Someone needs to investigate."

CHAPTER 11

But the thickening snow made it impossible for the drivers to climb the mountain.

"What about your baby mammoth?" asked James. "He actually seems to like this weather."

"But he can't talk," said Flappy. "How will he tell us what's going on up there?"

"Webcam!" said Dustin. "Just attach the camera to his head, and we can watch his progress on the big screen!"

"Hey—I'll direct!" said Myley. "There could be a movie in this!"

The mammoth was soon trudging up the hill through the blizzard. The drivers watched, but there was nothing to see until he got to the top of the mountain. There he found not an actual dragon but a giant *metal* dragon—spitting out snow by the ton!

And in the background, up a tree, they could just make out who was controlling it. None other than Warren "Wheelie" Wheelnut's evil twin brother, "Wipeout!"

"He's trying to sabotage the race!" said Dee-Dee.

The baby mammoth raced back down to the Wheelnuts and it was time for action!

Now, although the Wheelnuts were fiercely competitive in the race itself, when it came to someone *interfering* with the race they would happily team up … it was time for a plan!

But how to defeat a huge Snow Dragon?

The most obvious material they had to work with was all around them—snow, mountains of the stuff!

First of all they decided to build a ramp. Nutz and Boltz used their onboard computer to calculate the perfect size and angle.

Two cars would go up the ramp—the first would be the Flying Diaper—its job would be to distract the dragon and James knew exactly how ...

 ... by building a snowman on top of the car—and not just any old snowman, Dustin and Myley styled it! The Flying Snowman flew up the ramp and the Snow Dragon immediately spotted it.

With the dragon distracted it was the Dino-Wagon's turn to fly up the ramp.

 The Snow Dragon didn't know what had hit it as the Dino-Wagon blasted it with a burst of flames from the onboard volcano!

"Take that, you icy bully!" yelped Flappy. "Time to melt into the background!"

The metal dragon was melting and fizzing, its mouth bent to one side. It was still shooting out some snow, but it was now aiming at the top of the tallest tree behind it ...

Blasting snow right at the two villains!

"That's freezing!" screeched Wipeout. "This snow is getting right up my nose—literally!"

"Ha-ha-ha! It tickles!" chuckled Dipstick.

But as the Snow Dragon finally toppled over, Wipeout wasn't finding the situation funny.

"We need to get away from this cursed mountain," said the villain as they fell out of the tree and landed in a heap. "I'll stop this ridiculous race next time!" he screeched as they stumbled towards their helicopter.

CHAPTER 12

The Wheelnuts all cheered as the Dino-Wagon returned triumphantly. With no fresh snow falling, all it took was a mighty blast from the volcano to clear a path. The race was back on and the Wheelnuts were delighted.

"Give me ghosts over Snow Dragons any day," said Gurgle as the drivers jostled for position.

"Time for some REAL racing," said Campbell. "The road ahead is clear, there are no dragons, no ghosts … it's all about speeeeeed."

The Supersonic Sparkler was now in first place, the Wheel Deal right behind it and the Rust Bucket 3000 neck and neck with the Flying Diaper. But something wasn't quite right ...

"Grandpa, is it me or is the car going faster and faster and FASTER?" said James, who was having to hold tightly on to his seat.

"I do believe you're right," said Campbell. "We're no longer on a road—we're on a toboggan track!"

WHOOSH!

SKID!

The cars were slipping all over the frozen track, spinning around, bumping into each other!

"Use the brakes!" shrieked Boltz. But the Rust Bucket 3000 was zipping along and nearly out of control. The only car in control was the Wheel Deal.

"Check out the skates!" said Dustin. The two cheesy stars were wearing ice skates and guiding their car in a straight line.

"I just knew that our ice dancing experience would come in handy!" said Myley as they guided the limo.

But over in the Supersonic Sparkler Dee-Dee was madly checking their recently-delivered magic powders.

"Hair-Growing Magic Powder—no, Thirst-Making Magic Powder—no," said Dee-Dee. Then she spotted it. Super-Grip Grit Powder!

With the magic powder deployed the Supersonic Sparkler was again in the lead and heading to the next checkpoint!

VAMPIRE CAVE AHEAD!

CHAPTER 13

One by one the Wheelnuts drove through a gateway and into a huge cave. At first there was no sign of vampires.

VA-RoOM!

Behind the Supersonic Sparkler the other cars all roared through the checkpoint one after another.

The stars: 6 stars for first place, 5 stars for second place, 4 stars for third place, 3 stars for fourth place, 2 stars for fifth place and 1 star for sixth place.

VAMPIRE CAVE CHECKPOINT

1 Supersonic Sparkler ⭐⭐⭐⭐⭐⭐

2 Jumping Jalopy ⭐⭐⭐⭐⭐

3 Dino-Wagon ⭐⭐⭐⭐

4 Rust Bucket 3000 ⭐⭐⭐

5 Wheel Deal ⭐⭐

6 Flying Diaper ⭐

With the checkpoint scores on the board the racers had entered the final, and what felt like the scariest, part of the race! With no sky above, and only the occasional flickering light, the Wheelnuts had no idea what was around the next corner. The first team to get a sense of what was coming was the Dino-Wagon.

"There is some sort of creature in here," said Turbo Rex. "Something big and something not very friendly …"

Suddenly there was a loud whooshing noise, a screech and the first creature appeared. It was big and had vast wings and huge fangs …

"My onboard reading says Giant Vampires!" said Nutz. "And then some other stuff you don't really need to know about …"

"What other stuff?" said Boltz nervously.

"Oh … just that they have colossal appetites and have been known to attack caaaaaaaaars!!!"

Fortunately the vampires didn't like the look of the Rust Bucket 3000's tank-like frame, but the other cars weren't so lucky.

Giant vampires were now swooping down on all the vehicles, snapping and snarling and trying to take great bites out of them!

"Get your teeth off my antenna!" wailed Nelly as the Supersonic Sparkler tried to shake one off while trying to stay in the lead.

"They're dining on my diaper!" sobbed Burp. "Blast them with toxic wind!"

"Not the back wheel!" said James as a bat flew off with a great chunk of wheel in its mouth.

It was the Wheel Deal that finally worked out a way to get rid of the pesky bats by using their Gold Star upgrade.

"Fireworks display!" said Myley.

"That should scare the bats off," said Dustin— who just loved an excuse for sparkly fireworks.

The bats couldn't take the screeching fireworks and brightly colored explosions—blinking madly, they flapped away. The race was back on!

The Wheelnuts zoomed out of the Vampire
Cave and ahead they could see the finish line. The
Wheel Deal was in the lead, but the Rust Bucket
3000 was gaining on them fast. The other cars were
all limping along, having had chunks bitten out of
them by the vampires …

But as the checkered flag loomed into view the
Supersonic Sparkler made a final dash for the line,
overtook the Rust Bucket 3000 and sneaked just
ahead of the Wheel Deal …

CHAPTER 14

Crossing the finish line an inch ahead as the crowd went wild!!!

The other drivers pulled up, frozen, nibbled and thoroughly spooked, but delighted to have completed the course. And there to meet them was Warren "Wheelie" Wheelnut!

"Congratulations, Wheelnuts! The Spooky Smackdown is a race nobody will ever forget!" said Wheelie.

"Congratulations to you all," said Wheelie as he handed out trophies to the top three cars.

"In third place we have the Rust Bucket 3000—you get the Mummified Medal.

In second place is the Wheel Deal, you get the Blood-Curdling Cup.

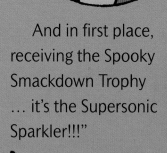

And in first place, receiving the Spooky Smackdown Trophy … it's the Supersonic Sparkler!!!"

Final Race Placings
1 Supersonic Sparkler
2 Wheel Deal
3 Rust Bucket 3000
4 Jumping Jalopy
5 Flying Diaper
6 Dino-Wagon

"We have a superspecial guest, international film director Steven Scorplanksi, with a special announcement," said Wheelie.

"A new star has emerged from this race who I want to appear in my next film," said Scorplanksi. Myley and Dustin, giggling, started to move to the front when they were interrupted. "You're going to be a **star**, baby mammoth!"

"Well that's all for this race," said Wheelie as the applause died down.

"Congratulations to our three trophy winners and don't forget you've all got lots of Wheelnut Gold Stars to spend in the Wheelnut Garage."

"I know what I'd like," said Dee-Dee. "I think these wings have frostbite— let's get some new, improved flappers!"

"Well don't forget the third race starts soon! Join us for Race 3 in the Craziest Race on Earth!"

Turn over for a sneak peek of the next course …